From the Movie

DISNEP
FROZEN
MAGIC OF THE
NORTHERN LIGHTS

A BRAVE BEGINNING

Written by Suzanne Francis

Illustrated by the Disney Storybook Art Team

PaRragon

Bath • New York • Cologne • Melbourne • Delhi
Hong Kong • Shenzhen • Singapore

Kristoff excitedly led his friends into Troll Valley. "Every year at the crystal ceremony, Grand Pabbie honours the young trolls who have earned all of their level-one crystals," he explained. "It's a huge achievement."

With each step, Queen Elsa's and Princess Anna's curiosity grew.
They couldn't wait to experience this mysterious tradition
for themselves.

"They're here!" Bulda said, when she saw the group of friends. The valley burst into life as trolls rolled out to greet them.

"Kristoff!" a young troll named Little Rock shouted, running to hug him. Little Rock was set to be in this year's ceremony. "I can't believe it's finally time!" he said.

"Can you tell us more about the ceremony?" Anna asked.

"It has to be performed during autumn under the Northern Lights. And we only have a few more days before the last night of autumn," Bulda said before repeating an old troll saying: "Guardians of Earth know autumn lights and crystals glow so our bond may deepen and grow."

Anna whispered to Elsa, "Did you understand that?"

Elsa shrugged. "Troll wisdom can be very confusing."

Anna noticed Little Rock holding several items in his hand. "I like your crystals," she said.

Little Rock proudly explained the meanings of each of his three glowing crystals.

"What about that one?" Anna asked, looking at one that wasn't lit at all.

"My tracking crystal," he explained. "It won't glow until I have excellent tracking skills. If I can't earn it, I can't be in the ceremony."

"But I don't understand," he continued. "I've been tracking all kinds of things, like caterpillars and insects."

"Little Rock," said Kristoff. "You need to venture out of the valley and use what you've learned. Tracking is more than just following."

But the idea of leaving the valley alone made Little Rock nervous.

"To be a good tracker you need to be fearless, be observant, and even be inventive sometimes," said Kristoff. "I know you can do it."

"I'll try," said Little Rock. "But I'm not sure –" Suddenly he gasped. "Look at those clouds! If we can't see the Northern Lights, there won't *be* a ceremony!"

Then he looked around for Grand Pabbie ... but the old troll was nowhere in sight. None of the other level-one trolls were there, either! "Where is everyone?" Little Rock asked nervously. "Did they forget me?"

"Don't worry," said Bulda. "I'm sure Grand Pabbie just went to find a new site where the lights are visible."

"Why don't we track him?" suggested Kristoff. "Maybe you can earn your crystal."

Little Rock's frown spread into a smile. "A REAL tracking quest? With all of you? Yes!"

"That could be a long trip," said Bulda. "You'd better take some warm cloaks so you don't get cold!" Quickly, the trolls dressed Anna and Kristoff in cloaks of moss and leaves. Elsa politely declined because she never felt cold.

As they started off, Elsa pointed out wisps of Northern Lights in the distance. "Maybe we should head that way?"

"That's what I was thinking!" said Little Rock, as he hurried to take the lead.

When the path split three ways, Little Rock froze. He looked back at Kristoff helplessly.

Kristoff pointed to the first path. "That goes *back* to Troll Valley," he hinted.

Little Rock stepped towards the second path.

"That's towards Arendelle," said Anna.

He confidently started down the third path. "This way!"

Suddenly, Little Rock stopped. "I'm picking up a scent."

"Trolls have an incredible sense of smell," Kristoff whispered to the others.

"I think it's Grand Pabbie!" Little Rock dropped to the ground and began sniffing along a trail ... straight to a hoof.

"Um, that's Sven," Kristoff said gently.

Little Rock tried to cover his mistake with a joke. "Sven! Stop standing on Grand Pabbie's footprints!"

Elsa could see that Little Rock was nervous, so she thought a story might be just the thing to ease his mind. "The Northern Lights make me think of the amazing beauty of nature," she said as they continued up the mountain. "What do the lights make you think of, Anna?"

Anna smiled at her sister. She knew exactly what Elsa meant.

"One night, long ago," began Anna, "our parents took us to the top of a huge mountain, hoping we'd get a great view of the Northern Lights."

"We had never been up so high," said Elsa.

"Or up so late!" added Anna.

"We were playing hide-and-seek under the light of a full moon until, suddenly, these pink and green ribbons of light rippled across the sky," said Anna.

"The Northern Lights!" exclaimed Olaf.

"Yes!" said Anna. "Then we ran up a steep hill to get higher!"

Elsa smiled. "Actually, I used my powers to make a staircase out of snow! It was like we were running up into the sky."

"When we reached the very top, a snow flurry fell around us,"
said Anna. "Sitting there together with the lights and the stars
and the glittering snow...."

"It was amazing," Anna and Elsa said together.

"See, Little Rock?" said Elsa. "New experiences may be scary at first, but if you're fearless, they can turn into fun adventures!"

As the group reached a frozen river, Kristoff reminded everyone to walk carefully. "I don't know how solid the ice is."

"Don't worry," said Little Rock. "I did complete my ice trekking crystal. And this is definitely thick enough –" CRACK!

The ice split beneath Little Rock's feet! Anna and Kristoff grabbed him but they struggled to hold him up because he was so heavy.

"Elsa! Remember the story? Maybe a stairway can get us across," Anna shouted.

Elsa quickly got to work. The group watched as a swirl of ice began to form into a stairway arching over the river.

They ran up the steps, but when they started to descend they heard a rumble. The riverbank beneath Elsa's stairway began to break off.

"I don't know what to do!" Little Rock cried. "I think this is a level-two crystal challenge!"

Thinking fast, Elsa waved her arms. Sheets of ice appeared and when their fronts curled up and froze, they looked like sledges! "Jump on!" Elsa shouted.

Everyone swooshed down the steep arch. Picking up speed, they raced down the frozen river.

As the sledges slowed to a stop, the friends whooped happily. They had made it across the river.

Little Rock smiled up at Elsa and Anna. "You saved us! I want to be fearless just like you," he said. He gave them a glowing crystal from his pouch. "You deserve to carry this."

Elsa and Anna admired the beautiful crystal.

Determined to be a fearless leader like his friends, Little Rock declared, "This way to Grand Pabbie!"

"That's back to the river," whispered Kristoff.

Little Rock spun around. "I meant this way!" he said, marching in the opposite direction. The others smiled and set off to follow the distant glow of the Northern Lights, ready to face whatever adventures stood between them and the crystal ceremony.

They were sure Little Rock would find Grand Pabbie and the Northern Lights, and get his tracking crystal to glow – even if he did need a little help along the way!